Mark Getty was born in Rome in 1960. He grew up between there and Siena. He has four children, three grandchildren, seven dogs and two donkeys. In 1995 he co-founded Getty Images; from 2008–16 he served as Chairman of the National Gallery.

Today he lives between Rome and Oxfordshire with his partner Caterina and their daughter Sol.

This is his first book.

MARK GETTY

LIKE
WILDFIRE
BLAZING

ADELPHI

First published in 2018 by Adelphi Publishers

Text Copyright © Mark Getty, 2018
Endpages and bird on the case © are drawn by the author, 2018

This edition © Adelphi Publishers, 2018

The title *Like Wildfire Blazing* comes from Robert Fagles' translation
of *The Iliad*, Book 2, part I, reproduced with permission from
Penguin Random House UK

ISBN 978 0 95623 879 5

A CIP catalogue reference for this book is available from the British Library

Typography and typesetting by Peter B. Willberg
Typeset in Goudy Modern

Printed and bound by CPI, Moravia

For my children Alexander, Joseph, Julius and Sol
and my grandchildren Jasper, Olivia and Gene

BOOK ONE

Once upon a time there was a dark forest which was so big it had no edge. It was also so dark that almost all living things inside it were colourless and only partially sighted. It was a place for the albinos of every species. One of these was old, had skin like scrunched up paper, and a tiny domed head to house a tiny domed brain. In the forest you didn't need a brain, instinct made you eat or starve, win or lose. He had instinct. He knew some things before they ever needed to get to a brain. Thus, in the dark dark forest he ate and won. He was a worm-man, and his name was Getto.

Outside the forest lived a machine race of super mammals, who were human above the waist, and goat below. They too would have been bathed in darkness, but they had created neon-gas lights up on the ceiling of their part of the universe and thus lived in perpetual half light. These things made things, and sold things, and exchanged things. They then wore things, drove things and did everything you can do with a thing. The ones who had the most things were the kings of this half world. Amongst them was their most king-like, most crafty thing-maker. He was called Ordög.

Of the two, Getto was the better schemer. He was simple and essential when it came to looking for someone's weakness. He also always avoided a rival's strength. His instinct was so strong that he could smell a weakness on someone's skin or breath within moments of knowing them. It's all he wanted of them; their key, their unlockable-you, their rifled treasure chest of self. They would never know what or how it was happening, but it was happening. He was the great and base hunter of id and ego; the emptier of minds.

Ordög was no such slippery troubadour. He was, after all, the thing king. He could hold and entrap time if he wanted. He wouldn't even need to get close. His fabricated world of metal would ensnare his prey without him even risking a heartbeat.

In between, and above, and on the sides and below, was another part of the planet. This was an ocean of light, an upland of warmth. Those in the dark forest and those in the machine world all wanted to have this place, which they called the Motherland. They thought only one being lived here and she was a she. She roamed around her world alone and did things, and saw things. She was the only pure thing in the known and unknown. She knew nothing of the forest or the machines, and knew only movement and laughter. But those in the forest, and those in the machine world knew of her. And they wanted to possess her. Not to have her and to hold her, but to vanquish any idea that there might be spirit in the universe. So, slowly, Getto and Ordög plotted apart to bring her to them. And vanquish life. Her name was Sol.

Sol flew in the Motherland, which needed only her, for in herself she had everyone, and thus needed no one. Sol was neither good nor bad, she was before both. Goodness and badness are only ever useful in celestial courts when they are used in small doses. In large amounts they are both banal. Before the law was handed down there was only a world like Sol's; it wasn't human, it was just music.

Getto and Ordög both came upon a plan at the same time. They would nab the bird. For Sol wasn't alone in the Motherland. Though she was the only goddess, there was one other creature: a bird called Papageno. In Getto's world of the dark forest there were plenty of blind colour-less birds and slippery bats. In Ordög's planetary machine shop there were no birds, though he had made some flying machines. The only true bird bird, as we would know a bird, was with Sol in her sky world of music and flight. Sol knew about the bird, but didn't befriend it.

So everyone in our tale was alone. Getto, alone. Ordög, alone. Sol, alone. And the bird Papageno, alone too. But only Papageno was lonely. Sol lived in her world of music. The others in worlds of dark and of bad. Only Papageno searched for talk, and for touch. Only Papageno was warm. And both Getto and Ordög knew this.

Papageno would sometimes fly to the boundary between the Motherland and the dark forest. Unnoticed by Sol, he wanted the simple warmth of bird-chat, the opening and closing of babble beaks, the talk of too much, and the mindless morning tongue-wag of life. He was like this, our Papageno, everyone's friend, and the other side of every noble and simple and silly conversation. Skirting the wilting trees at the forest's edge, Papageno would call out to his sad sick sightless cousins in a warm ray of voice. 'Birds; skypoems and skylarks, winged hearts, gather, for it's morning, and the world is once again alive.'

Thus, every morning flightless and crippled birds and bats would gather as the night's fear and gloom subsided to listen to Papageno's trilling sunshine of talk. On this occasion, as on all the others, everything seemed suddenly right with the sky and the land and the water. Except for the appearance at the edge of the forest of a pale frigid transparent and paper-thin worm-man, the milk of human unkindness himself: Getto.

The boundary between the sky and the forest beneath was permeable, but no one ever crossed it. Papageno would occasionally stray over the trees at the edge of darkness. But even he knew that he was from his world of light and not from the glowering dark. So he would bend his wing back to the light whenever he felt the chill from beneath the trees rise up and touch his spine. On this morning, having called out in his whistled joy to the creatures on the other side, he careered back and forth over the boundary. The wind felt like surf, the leaves scattered like schools of fish. And on and on he banked and rolled and slid as he slowed, then plunged for speed's thrill, and came up as the wind blew. It was as if each heaving breath of his was also leaving the woodland's lungs. As if they were one this time, it and him.

While Papageno soared and Getto plotted, Sol lived and loved in innocence. Without companions or demi-gods to gambol with, she played with clouds and stars and talked to herself of notes and tones, and sang songs made up of wind and fire and flowers. This was her morning song that morning:

> O broken light,
> Of fire kind,
> Waking finger bright,
> Touch my morning mind…

This she sang softly with the breeze, over and over as dawn poured out of the night. Sol was born alone, and lived alone. She knew nothing of other songs: songs of pain, and songs of love; people's songs of people's lives. She sang of what she knew, and for now she didn't know the heart and the way it breaks; she didn't know the laugh and how it ripples, nor the tear as it wets its way, nor the daily fear of death. None of this was in her songs yet. She sang of the universe, of the four elements, of the power of water, and the force of mountains; she sang of her love of gods and of the planets, and above all of the warmth of the sun. But she sang and sang. That morning she sang.

Listening to her sing wasn't simple, though it was divine. Papageno heard her and always flew towards the music but never got near it. Getto knew of it, but did not know it. Ordög, on the other hand, was the great base engineer of time and things. He had heard a high tone touch the edges of his world and measured the shape changing of his sky envelope. The sound produced by Sol was so pure and so perfectly pitched that it travelled further and faster than any other sound. When it reached the edge of the sky and touched the limits of his darkling country, it was as if the voice vibration embraced the blackening clouds and slightly tightened their own places of space and time. We all have a sudden and strange feeling sometimes that the world isn't what we think it is. An unexpected flash of light, a shadow cast by nothing, a sound in silence. We mostly ignore it and quickly look for the comfort of repetition. But not Ordög.

Ordög set sensors at all of his sky corners. In between them he ran small narrow ribbons of bubbled raindrops. As soon as Sol's voice tingled his cloud's outer envelope, the sensors stretched and the bubbled raindrops opened to release their cargo of water. Though transferred to another medium, the falling water carried her sound, and he heard its percussion. In this sound was everything. Not just parts of everything: the picking and choosing of bits of life we like or not. But everything; all life. And though it wasn't a people's song or a people's voice, it was divine. Ordög had to have it, and believed that with it he could break away from the relentless evil and the daily bad of his metal-making. He briefly saw love.

Ordög couldn't use love to love back any love left. He was new to it. To capture her and hold her, to hold also this new love, he would have to use his finest and oldest trait, and that was hate. Hate is manyfold but also simple. Ordög had always employed it well. He could hate at heat; at cold he could make hate hard. He could look hate across a space and rip the colours off a butterfly's wings. He could hate a mother's milk and turn it into an incestuous curdled curse. He could hate a smile so that it bled, and hate a flower in its bed. He hated large and small. All his success was born of hate.

Of course Ordög made things, he was the great thing king. The machine world he man-straddled was a great steaming workshop of thing-making. He was just he, and he was hate, but he was not alone in the making of things. A slave force of warped and broken beings laboured tirelessly in the factory fabric of his machine-tooled world. And hate animated every bolt and screw and lathe and joint. Each small marriage of metal to metal was another little victory for envy and accumulation, for having against not having. And all this was done by harbouring and mollycoddling unimaginable heartbursts of hate. Ordög wanted Sol, wanted her voice, her beauty and mostly that love he felt as strong and new. A rival to hate maybe. He also knew that hate never dies, whereas love is only ever strong if you give up everything else. And who would do that he said to himself? Love could escape his grasp if he failed, and forever illuminate the universe; forever be like a sun in people's hearts, or a burst of roses from their mouths. Or, if he caught it now, caught it early, love too would be just another sort of possession. Another thing.

Ordög knew that to trap Sol he would need to use the bird as bait, but he had never caught a bird before, nor thought of it. Now he thought of little else. He didn't know much about birds, but this one seemed quick. Occasionally he would spy Papageno flying right outside the thinner air of his habitat; banking and coasting, pitching and yawing. He seemed good, this bird. Catching him would require more than a net or a sky-coloured silk gauntlet. Eventually his craft produced the answer. Ordög modelled and built a made-cloud. To do this he employed his finest makers. They laboured for months to build a cloud sparse enough to encourage a risk-taking bird to want to fly into it, and thick enough to make him regret it. The main makers designed, but in fact Ordög had an army of foetus-shaped little makers making for them. Beyond them, millions of coal black little spiders, each with a single lustrous red eye, wove light-year lengths of the thinnest tensile white webbing from their throbbing guts. This vast dark army of whirring legs was set to work under the darkened neon of Ordög's warehouse world, so all anyone could see was a slow inhalation and exhalation of spider pulse, and the cycling power wheel of millions of tiny hairy black legs; and those eyes. The red that you thought had grown into one eye from many.

Slowly and quickly the cloud came together. The makers were organized hierarchically, with mere producers at the bottom edge of the social structure, and the designers and administrators at the top. The cloud could not be assembled piecemeal in Papageno's flight path, but needed to appear all of a sudden one morning. This was not a simple logistical feat. The leading designer makers worked closely together with Ordög on the storage and assembly issues regarding the cloud. Nothing like this had been built by Ordög before. Even the weapons developed and distributed during the various wars and battles which had pitched Ordög's world against the dark forest, in the distant past, had been much simpler than this. The worst of those wars, and the one that stretched Ordög's manufacturing minions the most, was the 'War of the Thousand Nights'. Millions bled and died on both sides, and many other millions made the arms used to punish each other. Generations were lost. But, not all was on the deficit side of the butcher's ledger. Ordög and the makers of things learned about new ways of joining things to others, and ways of producing more for less. One of these lessons learned was how to assemble complex structures. During the 'Thousand Nights', sky bridges and water tunnels had to be built and put in place by sappers overnight whilst a siege was going on. These bridges and tunnels were very large objects, and Ordög learned how to store them and deploy them as needed. The folding of large structures like bridges or buildings was what led to the success he had in the deployment of the cloud. Folding anything makes a large thing smaller. Small things, like napkins, or paper origami, or clothes, are folded every day. And the principle applies to large things as well. What Ordög did, which transformed the world of logistics and manufacturing and storage, was that he learned how to store things entirely into themselves until they disappeared. It was like dark matter being folded into a black hole. Basically an object would keep subtracting itself from itself until it appeared to no longer be there. Its operator could then reverse the process wherever and whenever he wanted. Armies thus no longer needed supply lines. It revolutionized warfare. So the designers built the web-self-consuming-and-reject-ing-orifice into the cloud. And it was ready to place in Papageno's happy happy path at a moment's notice. That moment was to be the very next morning.

Getto was also primed and ready. He had followed Papageno's flight path carefully and knew where and when to strike. Getto didn't have Ordög's silky silver analytic brain, but he had instinct, determination and verve. He knew the race did not always go to the swift, and he also knew of the virtue of staying still. Sooner or later the world comes to you. He had watched Papageno skirt above the last tall trees at the edge of the dark forest, and had listened to him bring sweetness and light to his warped birds and bats. He quaked and sickened at this. Centuries of pain had been accumulated by him to hold his creatures close. No happy bird would rob him of that. No, he would rob the happy bird of happiness, for all of endless time.

That bird would regret soaring thoughts and fellowship, would regret music and song, would regret freedom and love. Getto always won. Whatever the price, someone else had to pay; he always always won. This dumb and happy bird would be undone — like most of his victims — by goodness. Instead of a castle of filigreed web cloud and all that was involved in producing that, Getto needed a foil, or a decoy, and he had one in a tortoise called Troia. And that is what this tale at history's beginning, middle and end spun around; everything good and bad, the universe itself, and its tectonic physics, revolved around the coming together the next morning of a cloud, a bird, and a tortoise. This would define the future of future itself.

Slowly night let its cold grip of space go, and light pulled across the sky like a table setting; a patient daily gathering of wind, warmth and colour. Papageno set off for his alarum of joy, his skypoems for larks, his smiling mad happy malarkey. And slowly as the sun burst forth across all the land, his troupe of hapless unhappy weathered and unfeathered bird friends crawled out of the grime and mud of their dark huddled hovels and opened their ears and hearts to hear his song. At this moment, with light now much greater than dark, Ordög unfolded and expelled the cloud from within its own orifice, and Getto pushed Troia the tortoise to a spit of sand beyond the forest's edge. Papageno suddenly could see them both. And his fate was sealed.

Papageno was all goodness and didn't hesitate. He swooped down from his great height and landed in front of the tortoise. The tortoise looked at him, and a tear rolled down his cheek. Papageno understood something and picked up the tortoise as the underbrush of forest and weed and thicket at the beach's edge burst open, and a foul smelling pale sea lion of human warping reached out to grab them. No bird could ever fly like Papageno could, nor ever would. And to Getto's amazement and frustration and fury, Papageno and the tortoise were beyond his grasp in a second, and in two were high up in the blue sky. Getto shook the trees, the copse, the glade, the wood, the entire dark forest, with his spring-coiled scream. But it was all too late for him. Papageno and the tortoise were now miles above. And heading towards a cloud Getto had only just noticed.

Invitingly situated above where the Motherland met the dark forest, the cloud grew ever larger as Papageno and his hanging tortoise approached. Papageno loved flying. Flight was full and fly like life. He banked into the first broken wave of cloud, all gathered like a petticoat, then spun through some of the whorled openings and on into more of the periwinkled shafts of sky, shoal, and shape. This was his moment, his Alpha and Omega. He shot past a cloud castle, then barrel rolled out of reach of some wispy strand of mist, which crept towards him like a grasping glove. This roll was his apotheosis. For one blessed moment he and the tortoise and the sky, and all of nature, were one. Then the tortoise caught on a strand of Ordög's cloud claw, and stuck. Papageno was thrown out of kilter by the shuddering stop of his passenger, and swiftly plunged worldwards. From the ground Getto watched in disbelief as his hunted prey fell towards him, whilst from his vantage point beyond the cloud, just outside his own ether, Ordög sat stunned as he watched his trap close on a tortoise instead of on Papageno.

The tortoise was left stuck to the webbed cloud and Ordög proceeded to invert its expansion. Soon, sooner than seconds, he reached his hands out and cupped the tortoise to himself, as the mile wide cloud did an inward pop and vanished inside itself. He put the tortoise in a corner of his realm. His work was undone. And his rival had Papageno at his feet at the edge of his world. He, on the other hand, had a useless tortoise. And Sol was forever seemingly out of his grasp. His eyes rolled like slot machines as he coldly calculated his next move. Emotion wouldn't disturb him as it might have done Getto. Getto, though, had his prey on the sand beneath his blubbery feet, and this time his voice rang out like a church bell for joy. He picked up the ailing bird by its neck and headed under the first foliage and into the darkness.

Getto had won. Ordög had lost. Papageno was mindless and dreamless. And Sol was now in mortal danger. If this tale had continued like this we could wrap it up here; Sol would be captured by hate, and love would die. But, no one had really considered carefully the role of the tortoise. And he now rose to his full place in the tale of the origin of happiness and love.

But who was he? How can a tortoise pretend to be important in a story like this? This is a tale for gods and nymphs, and a race of stunted worms. It's about the big things: love, beauty, good and bad. It has Sol in it. That's almost like saying, 'enough said'. It has not one, but two fantastically evil beings in Ordög and Getto. And, of course, it has the bird of life too with Papageno. This story didn't really need anything else. After all, I am writing it, and I should know. But, life is endlessly strange and brilliant and funny, and sometimes tortoises will make an appearance. Let me tell you something about this tortoise. Beginning at the beginning.

Born forever ago, his name was Troia, because tortoises, like the huge horse in ancient Troy, contain life in a box. Troia came from a storied and noble family, which had shared eggs with the most important tortoise families. In his life leading up to his capture by Ordög he had been a model tortoise. Don't think of him as you have seen him so far; as a victim. Nothing could be further from the truth. But now? Now he was cast off in a corner of Ordög's nightmare land of steam and clanging bursts of ear noise. Never expect speed from a tortoise, but in this one, Troia, expect everything else.

Troia the tortoise had surprising resources; many of them. But the most surprising of them all was that he could leave home. Now that shouldn't surprise any of us non-tortoises because we leave home all the time. But a tortoise's home is a tortoise. How can you leave home when home is you? Well, Troia could. And that's just what he did. At dawn on the second morning of his captivity he slid this way and that inside his shell, and then that way and this, and then once more this way and that. And suddenly he was out. Troia arranged his now empty home to look like a still fully functioning tortoise home, and crawled away to look for complete darkness in order to think and plan. Meanwhile, in the dark forest Papageno woke up to find himself also a prisoner, and not in a gilded cage. He was manacled at the ankle by a chain that could have held a merchant ship fast to a pier. And he was just a small bird. But that's how things go in this funny world of ours; nothing is what it seems.

And what about Sol? Hers was the only life that was not upturned by the universal hunt for her very life. She sang alone, not needing, not wanting, not pining, nor ageing or wilting, or sadly expecting life's locked and loaded two barrels of loneliness. She soared above, we pined below. She saw all things in their complete state, we see only their component pieces, and have to imagine the whole. We, who are not she, have little notion of what it means to see life whole like that. Sometimes we can catch a glimpse of it. It's momentary for us, and makes us gulp fistfuls of air as we realize that we had a small peek at a large revelation. Sometimes music can be our medium for this act of look-ing beyond experience, sometimes poetry, and sometimes – probably most times – it's the unexpected that stops us in our tracks. But not Sol. She witnessed and breathed in the roughest and rawest versions of fully formed life. Not our condensed version edited down by physics and chem-istry, but the all stream of consciousness total of it. That was her fate, to see life from the outside in. We saw what we saw, but thank the gods it wasn't that. In spite of all this Sol did notice that something was not right about the Motherland on a particular morning. She could not place what the difference was, but it was there. An absence of something. It was as if someone had let the air out of her planet. Everything became smaller fast. For the first time since forever began Sol lost her equilibrium. So she flew towards a hissing sound at the edge of her world, like the squeal of air being let out of a balloon, and closed in on her boundary with the dark forest. Good would not come from this.

As she careered closer and closer to her enclosed sky's edge, her flight uncompassed itself and she began to spin around her own tight orbit faster and faster. Soon, the breach in her sky's skin became a yawning sink hole of ejected life. She struggled with every sinew of muscle and tissue to change her headlong fall through this hell hole but her body could not fight it. She tried screaming out to her gods to intervene, but at this point no sound could escape the vortex of evacuating everything. Sol was in a plane-tary self-suction collapse. If she fought it she would die, and if she went with it she would likely die. She looked up above her and saw a rotating drum of unravelling planet collapsing upon her. The cylinder tightened. The noose was wound around another turn. She saw forests and lakes and mountain ranges and dreams and hope all turned into thin lava strings of crunched and compressed gravity screwed lifelessness.

And then she saw it. Way above her, maybe a moon away, but falling straight and true, like a ballistic dart, was a shaped heft of stone. Unburnt and untouched by its surroundings, it fell faster and faster towards the nar-rowing gap beneath her. Sol saw in a blink-moment that this dart might save her. She pitched her body towards the gap, breathed in, shut her eyes. A sound and a shudder accompanied her through. But she was through, and the thicker air this side of the deflating world she left caught her and let her stabilize. Only moments later the rock that hurtled at light speed through space shot into the gap and plugged it. She looked up at it, and saw that it was Amun Ra's great obelisk from the Temple of Karnak, and she breathed once again.

While Papageno and Sol now found themselves in a new place, one clearly a captive, and one a refugee, Troia had been thinking and planning in the half quarter light of Ordög's warehouse world. A tortoise plan was never going to take anyone by surprise; it was not going to be suddenly liberating and quickly just. It was slow; like liberation and justice. If you think about it for more than a few moments it becomes apparent that any riotous plan to overthrow a settled state of things must be based on speed and surprise. Speed and surprise were two attributes that Troia could not call on. All that was left were the other two timeless weapons of all conflict: strength and deception. Troia was a strong tortoise. Any other tortoise would attest to this. By any measure Troia could outdo other tortoises in any test of tortoise strength. Bench-pressing, log-tossing, tug-of-tortoise, in any of these he would prevail. But these were all games and trials at the intraspecies level. Try these against a field mouse or a pied kingfisher and the outcome would end up very differently. Let alone a brown bear or sea lion. So deception was the only weapon left to Troia. Now Troia was crafty, and could leave home and find home again, and most importantly had endless patience. And this is what he used. Quietly he crawled on his soft belly for many miles to a position where he could watch Ordög dictate instructions to the many makers in his thingdom. He would then crawl just as carefully back to where his shell lay as an empty Trojan deception and fill it briefly with tortoise truth. The rare inspection confirmed his own imprisonment within himself and gave him latitude to sneak and peek around Ordög's vicious little world without himself being sneaked on or peeked on.

Moving around was difficult, particularly as he had to return constantly to his grim corner and feign sleep, or hunger and thirst. But, slowly, he learned the geography of this part of Ordög's world. The makers worked most of the time and slept little, if at all. But when they did, they made their way out of the clanging factory forums, and shuffled in long tired dark queues towards raked and mildly depressed plots at the river's edge. As each of them got to their numbered place, they dropped into a falling foetal spoon and slept. As they slept, the tide of this murky slow-moving river would swell to the edge of each sleeping plot and fill the concave water bed with wet industrial waste. Phosphorescent mercury lit each bed like a child's reading light beneath a blanket, and lit the sleepers too, so that when they woke and walked they were like so many moving candles. This is what allowed Troia to find his way about this otherwise dark world. Day after day he followed these half-lit bodies from corner to corner. They never noticed him as he wasn't lit, and he learned all of the places that he needed to know, and some of the secrets which would cost him his life if they discovered that they were now known beyond them.

After a couple of months of moving about like this, Troia found a way out, and understood a great strength of Ordög's. He had been aware for some days that he was getting closer to something important and central to the thing maker's world. More and more of Ordög's larger foetus-shaped luminescent makers gathered in longer queues going back to work from their silvery sleep, and more and more darkened beings shuffled away at day's end to the river's edge.

Troia wondered at first whether these dark makers were different from the spectral lit wicks walking in at dark dawn. He thought there must be an inexhaustible supply of labourers of both the lamp light, and the dusk dark kind. It was only when he got very close, close enough to touch, that he realized that they were one and the same beings. At day's start they were full of milk white light from their viscous bath, and many hours later they were dusk and dusty dark; powdered black, no wax sheen, just a gritty grated pore stopping shale colour: coal. That was it. They were covered in coal dust, hiding the sickness of their mouth-filling mercury, by the sickness of their walking anthracite coffins. It made sense to Troia. The machines and their power had to have a prime mover. And coal was the answer. Ordög was either mining coal in industrial quantities or importing it from somewhere else. Troia would find the answer, and thus find Ordög's weakness. Because every great strength lies close beside a mortal weakness.

In the very middle of the forest, several days' walk from where Papageno had crumbled at the forest's edge, was Getto's nerve centre, and the dark heart of his dead empire. This is where he had Papageno held. There was no need for a cage. There was no way out for a bird whose feathers had been carefully plucked each by each, and hung together in a loose formless coat, along with many thousands of others, on the external walls of Getto's great forest fortress. This was the only colour anywhere in this murky jungle. So little light penetrated to these depths beneath the thick canopy that even this colour was rarely seen. But when it was, it dazzled the hopeless wan world, and lit every tiny faint heart with a moment's heartlumped fantasy. One ray of sun, just one, could pick out a rainbow of fanned and satinsilk bird majesty. None of this adorned a single bird anymore. Getto had stripped each bird clean of nature's greatest self-compliment, and reversed the favour onto himself. The world, for Getto, was a playground about him, for him, of him. And life, a game and a sport for him to play at, and for him to win. And death, well death was for all the others. He would see to that.

Sol had landed on the same spit of sand which Papageno had been taken from. She looked out to the sea and saw its great still blue blanket. Then she looked skywards to where she had come from and she saw a vestigial world, ruined, and no longer cocooned around her flight, but anchored now to land piers, with sky and land now stapled at the horizon. Her eyes adjusted to her immediate surroundings. Dark forest. Everywhere. Dark dark forest. Her old world was noble and painted by angels. Her new world looked frightening and ignoble. But Sol was new too. Her fall had been from grace, but also from herself. Her lonely Olympian domain had given her too much a serving of God, and too little a helping of man. Here that changed. Sol would fly less, sing less and she would solve the trials of men; one by one, as they came up. She turned her back to the sea and the sky and walked into the forest.

Her first encounters were with the various birds and bats who had come this far firstly to listen to Papageno's life lute, and her first ever conversation was with a bat who told her, to her great surprise, about the bird from her world, who was now a prisoner in this one. The difficulty would be finding Papageno to release him from his imprisonment, and thus began her new walk in life, and to bring her unreal universal love to a real need, and a real heart. But the way would be long and painful. And it began here. With this bat. 'You will never find him on your own', said the bat. She insisted, 'I can walk until I am far from here'. The bat answered, 'you are not blind, or subdued by a life of radar fear. You won't find him. But I will help you.' She asked how, and he told her and she fell to the floor, poleaxed by the first pain she had ever felt. For this is what he told her and planned:

I am a pale sick thing,
Not a bird in the sky,
A tattered glove as a wing,
And an ear for an eye.
By night I live, bugs die,
It's ever thus with bats.
With gnats and bugs, who also fly,
It's also thus; consuming selves, and dying like rats.
So it goes, round and round,
We wait, we kill, we die,
But now, with you, it's love I found,
And if death can love you back, it's mine.

So he told her that bats, when dying, emit a small light

45

from their failing hearts, and this would help guide her forth. The way was long and would need more than one light. But there was more than one bat. And he called them. And they came. They had lived hate, and would now die love. The dark forest path was now lit by a thousand tiny deaths. So Sol walked as in daylight to the heart of Getto's world.

What Troia found as he slowly slid belly front mud slip-
ping his tortoise turned bowl-less soup of self around
Ordög's night factory was a surprising sight, and a way
away. After weeks of hustling and bustling forth and
back from his shell elsewhere, and following a walking
cemetery of lit labour, he came across what at first was
just a warm breeze. He stopped, and pulled away from
the glow of the path. For an hour he waited hunched in
the darkness for this river of radioactive foetal cripples to
pour out beyond him. When the last one passed he inched
forward moving towards the source of the breeze. It was
now completely dark, but he didn't need light, because
the breeze soon stiffened and after that became sustained,
and then was no longer breeze, but wind. And he looked
up and knew why. Now there was a faint glow above him.
As if dawn was cracking open its coffin lid on this dark
and dusky plain. There was an opening the size of a house
at the sky's edge. He climbed up towards it as it got lighter
and lighter, and when he crested its sill, he saw it. Slowly
and majestically beating its broad wings against the strong
wind, like a sail that snaps full after luffing long, was a
glorious flying donkey.

The ass Bucephalus, the flying beast of burden. Nothing in Troia's eye-life had ever so suddenly been so beautiful. Ugliness and grace in harmony: the gods' final acceptance of things as they aren't. A flying ass seen by a flat tortoise. That's what all fiction should be. But this was not fiction, and Troia was a real tortoise caught in a moment of blinding beauty. He soon stopped his reverie and looked more closely at the donkey as it moved above and beyond him. On the donkey's back, strung from a halter just behind his wings, were two balancing bags open at the top and thick with coal. The donkey was now past him and through the sky window. Troia looked out again at space. A mile or so away he caught sight of something moving. He held his gaze there, and waited. It was moving. And it was coming towards him. And after a moment it was clear what it was. And it was another flying ass. And it too was carrying coal. And behind it, in space too, also a mile or so behind this one, was another. And behind it, again, another. And another. Through space, almost forever, stretched out a daisy chain of donkeys.

So Troia understood as he hung at the sill of this world what poetry was, and it was these winged donkeys, and what prose was; the donkeys' labour. And he also understood how Ordög furnished himself with fuel to build his fantasy of empire. Most importantly he now knew how to break Ordög's heart, and escape this place too.

Troia made his way back down from the sill, and back down the escarpment into the growing darkness, and eventually back to where he had left the queue of stunted sack flesh. At day's end they started filing past him again. Only this time they were black with coal. He nimbly joined their clumsy coal-dust column and walked in the dark to their home by the river. Here he made an appeal to those closest to him. He offered them freedom, and a new world. In exchange he needed help to unravel this world. Though tired, and eager to lie down and die a little in their tidal pools of poison, they listened.

Troia grew more eloquent as his rage grew. He told them they would have to fight for freedom. And that they would know continuing pain and privation, but it would be theirs. That they would know hunger, thirst, blindness, and despair, but it would be theirs. That they would inherit their own misfortunes, live with their own tragedies, give birth to their own disappointments, and die soon, or later, their own deaths, but it would all be theirs. And from it, some of them, would find the acorn of self, and from that, perhaps, the sapling of confidence, and for a few of them, eventually, the tree of manhood. But to get there, from here on this desolate and bleak and blank land, they would have to fight, and fight hard, and fight now.

Just as he finished his breathless speaking, a scratchy tinny tannoy sound all around and everywhere too, rang out like a medieval alarum. 'Attention, Attention. A prisoner has escaped from Far Corner 27. All work is suspended for the time being, and all workers, except those required to maintain system buoyancy, must report to their Section Fez for instructions, and for assignments to the appropriate hunting party.'

Troia knew where Far Corner 27 was, and he knew where he was now. He knew more about the geography here than most anyone. There was little doubt in his mind that most of the attention of the search parties would be focused on that section. He could therefore lead his new army towards the coal depots with little fear of finding a force to stop him. So, without hesitating, he led his darkened troops away from the dead silvery river and into the darkness on his way to swiftly slice an open sluice in Ordög's unwary ankles. However Ordög never let a moment be just a moment. And this was no exception. As soon as he heard that Troia's shell had been found empty he prepared for the worst. Yes, he was just a tortoise, but for how long had he been missing, and for how long had he been snooping around, and what had he learned? Ordög couldn't afford to lose a single secret. He wasn't a witch, or a magus whose secrets were sealed around themselves. Ordög's secrets were different in nature. They were corporate in nature, and linked in chains like the manufacturing they were designed to conceal. The discovery of one would reveal the next and the next after that. And so on. So Troia was dangerous to him and he lost no time in girding his world to war.

Troia and his troops arrived at the coal depots to find them lightly defended. He needed to overwhelm the guards quickly and set charges, as well as prepare for the withdrawal and escape of himself and thousands of foot soldiers. He remembered what he could of the rules of war. But mostly he just made do by deciding things on the spot without reflection. In the first instance he could not trust his raw recruits to execute his instructions faithfully. So he had to do things himself. His advance force killed the perimeter guards. Then, once inside the facility, they killed everyone in the administrative offices. Troia then found the coal-fired steam engine that ran both the plants' machines. He gathered all of the combustible material he could find and began to send individual soldiers out with burning torches to coal tailings around the entire plant. They started lighting them.

The situation was now critical. Ordög's troops would see the flames and return to the depot in force. So Troia needed to defend an escape route to the open sky window. He did this by defending not one, but two escape routes. One was heavily and obviously defended. The other lightly and unobtrusively. He placed his worst troops at the former, and sprinkled his best at the latter. The fires were now raging across the massive power plant. Coal was burning everywhere. The troops were deployed across the perimeter and along the escape routes. He was ready. And it was a good thing he was, because Ordög now came down on him like a rainstorm of bustling, screaming, bleeding, hacking death.

First Ordög sent in the spiders. Millions of them poured over the sand berms surrounding the entrance areas of the plant. Troia had his first line of defence here. The spiders overwhelmed it. Anyone in their path was soon covered by spiders and their bites. As the spiders stuck to Troia's troops like a new skin, the coal dust that had covered them since they returned from this very depot earlier in the day fell away. Now they were translucent again but covered by moving patches of black spiders. From where Troia stood all he could see was this shadow play of spastic squirming soldiers, now dark, now light; some of them spinning to run from the pain, and as they spun the light would spin too, and spiders in clumps would fly off the rounding, shaking and flayed bodies. Troia withdrew his remaining frontline troops to behind the second berm. This berm had a channel on both sides, and each of these was full of burning coal. As Ordög moved his front line forward he sent the spiders to the second berm. They raced over the sand as a black moving mass. There were so many that you could hear them before you could see them; a drum roll of spider legs.

The first few yards of spiders in the first channel on the outer side of the second berm burned to thick black paste. Surviving spiders raced above their sticky kin, and up, above, and over the berm. Here they ran into the second burning channel of coal. There were sufficient spiders to choke the channel with another hecatomb of pasted spider, but not enough to see through the battle. Ordög sent them to their deaths knowing that a species was dying. He kept one with him though. This was one of the senior designer spiders, and one whom nature had designed as a self-satisfying, one-in-all procreating onanist. If Ordög survived, and this one spider survived then there would be spiders again wherever one turned one's head.

The second berm was crossed by Ordög's shock troops. The battle front was narrowing. Troia's inexperienced recruits were fighting bravely, but dropping back fast. Soon they were fighting hand to hand in a narrow strip of coal dust at the intersection of Troia's two lines of retreat. The burning channels were dying down now. The outer coal tailings had burned and those fires too were mostly snuffed out. The only real blaze left was behind Troia on the large tailing against the old quarry wall.

And now, in front of this raging conflagration Ordög appeared on the battlefront. He moved purposefully towards what he could see in front of him. And what he could see in front of him was Troia. And Troia could see him, and moved towards him, knowing now that his great-est deception needed to be flawless if he were to survive.

As he moved towards Ordög, Troia gave his remaining forces the order to retreat along the second path. At the same time he ordered his troops defending the first path to make it appear as if a lot of activity was occurring on that road. The battle was now being fought for fighting's sake only. The outcome was decided already. Ordög's sacrifice of his spiders had turned the day to him. All he wanted now was to slowly slide his blade across this tortoise's throat, and watch the blood spill to the floor as barren seed. Troia knew that he would have to run the risk of dying easily if he was to carry out his plan; and the risk was great. But Troia was Troia. And Ordög was about to find out just how surprising this irritating tortoise could be.

Troia moved first. Slowly. Ordög slipped his blade from its sheath. When he planted it in him, he thought, this tortoise would be its new sheath. The noise around them was deafening as soldiers around them lived for moments only, and only to think briefly about how to kill, before they too died. The flames flickered in a lifelike dance of the world's end. But, inside the circle of fire and sound and death, Ordög and Troia circled a narrower path around each other's lives, and all sound was absent; there was just movement, a dangerous ballet of death. Ordög toyed first, swinging his blade as if it was no more than an essay in bladecraft. Troia moved like a man does at his first dance lesson, deliberately, but not well. And then it all happened quickly and suddenly. Ordög swung the blade with every-thing he had behind it. Too much. Troia surprisingly moved towards and not away. The force of Ordög's arms, and the kinetic power unleashed, did knock Troia hard. But he now was so close to Ordög that he could clutch him. And he held fast. Ordög swung and swung, but couldn't swing him off. When Troia regained his balance, he just leaned into Ordög hard, looked at his cold eyes, crawled up and reached into Ordög's pocket with one hand as he held on to him with the other. In this pocket he felt a small metal box with a single protruding button. And this button spelled the end of Ordög's world. It operated the cloud. He pressed the button.

What happened next was hard for those involved to fathom. Harder still for those who died instantly as the cloud stretched and popped into its full girth inside the warehouse world, and not outside as was intended. This would have been bad under any circumstances, but, with a raging fire on the eastern escarpment, it was dire. The cloud expanded fast and compressed every living and inanimate object within into ever smaller versions of themselves. What was big got small, and what was small got smaller. Everything being relative should have meant that this would be no problem for a big balloon with a small balloon growing fast in its innards. But not everything is relative. Not everything works the same way small as big. Take the heart; love animates it, but oxygen, and valves, veins, and blood keep it running. As everything got smaller the unexpected happened. The oxygen carried by the now smaller blood cells refused to play the game of tiny and tiny again. So the blood cells going through the aorta carried more and more oxygen, and less and less blood. Soon their hearts were like so many gaping mouths trapped inside expanding rib cages, and they exploded inside them, as they bustled and jerked their last breaths. The lucky ones were those already at the sky window, and those including Troia and Ordög and the last remaining spiders, which were at the point of impact. They were immediately shot through the window as the cloud expanded to fill the last corners of Ordög's world. The great fire licked its way up the escarpment as its increasing confinement channelled it upwards. It was now a fire separated from its coal base, as it snaked its way to find more fuel. And it did. In its last weight gain of expansion the cloud pushed a rivulet of flame to the window sill's edge overlooking empty space. The high wind forcing its way in caught the fire and spread it like a sun spot. In an instant Ordög's world was blown to bits.

The explosion was universal and even cracked space. It left scars still visible today. It also pushed everything at the sky window and just outside it deep into space. Surviving foetuscs who had taken the second path were now floating in space. Machines too were lying at clumsy angles in voids. Flying donkeys were floating fireballs of wings and legs all akimbo. And, at a low bass register, you could hear angry, confused, stubborn and braying, like whale song in the deep. It was onto these last living donkeys that our heroes and villains and remaining troops climbed for the long journey to their new home in the dark forest.

As she stepped over the last strobe lit bat and into the opening outside Getto's fortress, Sol saw a rainbow wrapped around the walls. She was used to beauty, but not like this. Every boulder was braided, each crack cushioned, the four gates gathered, and turrets trestled with feathers. The fortress walls shimmered as the little light played on them, and as a gentle breeze swept through the woodland glade, the fortress shape shifted like stippled and speckled sea salmon under rippled water.

Sol moved to the gates, which she found open, and passed through. She was now in Getto's lair. She had seen nothing like it. It was her first sight of a built place, where door led to street, and street to square, and square to trade and talk. She wouldn't know this, but it had the look of the great Zulu capital of Ulundi, home of Shaka and Dingane; or of the hilltop settlements on the Aventine and Quirinal of Remus and his lupine twin Romulus. They were beginnings of something. Not cities, nor even towns yet, but not camps either. And this place too was more than a lair, more than a cliff face cave, dark enough and deep enough to drag back the bodies from a hunt, pull them in, and watch time, digestion, and teeth turn them from pink flesh to calcium bone. No, though this place still hung with the ancient stench of dried blood, it was also a place where Sol could make goodness from base bad.

61

Sol moved towards the centre of this strange place, and there she saw what she was looking for. A bright, smiling, daylit and featherless bird looked long at her from his broken captivity. He then smiled long, and blushed. They both moved towards each other, and when they met in the middle of Getto's fortress, Sol bent over and picked up Papageno's broken and raked body. His eyes smiled like a baby's trust. She held him close, and briefly sang her song he knew so well. And as she sang it the dark woods around the forest with all of its background hum, ceased to make noise at all, as all ears strained to pick out this god-strain of sun singing. As she sang the air around the fortress stilled, the forest damp rose, the light lamped down and in, from the high thick canopy, which now seemed to open and part. And as the sunlight floated down to the forest floor it found the sun song and they merged into moving song light. And then the walls of the forest fortress began a slow upward snowflake rise of first one, then feathers all, floating one by one, to birds in the trees, and in nests, and roosting, and feeding their chicks, and wetting their beaks. To each a first feather fell in place, then slowly all. In her arms Sol watched Papageno as she sang her lullaby, and watched as his magical coat of feathers found its way to warm and fly his bird self. And when she stopped, everything stopped; sound, movement, even the play of light. A miracle had happened. The world had to stop. And then, because it was the world, it unstopped and went on. Birds burst into flight, brooks babbled, and fish chased after mayfly. Life began.

BOOK TWO

Three days after they set off, leaving Ordög's world all broken and unbridled behind them, Troia, Ordög, the spider, and a few hundred soldiers made landfall at the far side of the dark dark forest. The surviving flying donkeys set them down where they had always set themselves down to bear their next load up, and that was at Getto's open cast coal mine.

After all that had happened, and fearing all that would, Troia and Ordög just focused on finding water and something to eat, before thinking about resuming their hostility. Ordög's dark metal world was gone, as was Sol's Motherland, and now only the dark forest remained. And remaining with it were all of our tale's friends, both good and bad. They had lit up the night sky with their deeds, and their industry. Their evil made space strings and black holes, their bravery, mass.

But now they were all here; a gathering of faults and virtues on this stepping stone to something. So they hunkered down for now. Drank from streams and ate from the bounty that Getto had left untended in the woodland's midst. And occasionally in these first days of peace and recovery they would look up at where they had been, and would see comet trails of still flaming debris and burned out husks of rock. If they looked further they could see slowly spinning strings of orbiting dead foetuses, and flying donkeys frozen in place by the lungfuls of jet flame they inhaled at the sky window. They were all points of light now. And one day would be stars. They looked down again and drank the clear water of the running brooks and creeks of this new home.

Troia was the first to organize. He gathered his force and fed them. When they regained some of their strength he moved himself and them far from the mine to a bluff overlooking the sea. And here they built a palisade first, then inside they raised roofs over their needs. On one side the bluff and the sea protected them, on the other the tightly bound wooden stanchions of the palisade. Troia had once been here and was then but a tortoise. In Ordög's warehouse world he was first a prisoner, then a scout, then a terror tortoise, and finally a battle leader of an army. Here he was beginning to be that next thing in the lifeline of those we call great, a civic leader; a tortoise Pericles. He divided the community into those who do this and those who do that. He made hewers of water hew, and bailers of hay bail. He made his best soldiers better. And those who could write and dream and draw he brought close to him. And had them tell the story of who they were, and where they came from. And slowly this palisade with its seasons of plenty, and its wit and store against seasons of less, became a place that would still be there when you next looked. And they called it Polimnia, after poetry and beauty. Over time, with sustenance, light, and learning, the crippled foetal forms of his volunteers uncracked their handicap and became half-men.

Getto had been squat splayed on the far sand spit waiting to see how many of his donkeys would return from the star burst he witnessed at night. Over the three days he watched a paring knife strip off his great rival's world like hunks of hanging blubber sheared clean from a live whale's harpooned still life. He watched and allowed himself to laugh. And then he strained his eyes for his train of flying donkeys. Getto had a huge investment in his coal mine and in his donkeys. His hate for Ordög was great, but his fear of losing so much trade was great too. And, as his eyes picked the space in space where he expected donkeys, something else blurred in flight over him. He swaddled his grey corpse into lard-like attention, and looked again; this time not out to space, but closer, here, above the trees. And he saw them: birds. With feathers. Beautiful flying acres of colour. Without thinking again of space and coal and his long train of flying donkeys he pitched into the forest smartly. Knowing that if his birds had feathers and flight he would eventually be grounded and flayed. Things were that simple. Either you or I would win, never both. And winning always meant a little, but losing meant everything. Headlong into the dark he rushed.

As he stumbled through lanyards and vines in the gloom on the forest floor Getto felt a spongy resistance beneath his feet and thought they were mushrooms. All the better. It made his usually lumbering progress nimbler; at times he felt light and quick as he pushed off a thick mushroom with one of his fat feet. Now he was practically flying through the forest, bouncing horizontally along the path's twists and turns. It was not only quick now, but fun. He felt giddy and lightheaded. He had laughed this morn- ing, but that was at someone's pain. It was much the only laughter he knew. But now he laughed a new laugh of joy, of sheer happiness. Getto was laughing out loud, and happily. And even the thought of birds with their feathers didn't seem so awful. And their bird song seemed to match his happiness, not scratch and scrape like it always did. And he thought too now, as he got closer to the clearing in front of his forest fortress, that Papageno should be free to spread the sort of joy he was feeling now, as he ball- bounced childishly into the first inkling of light at the clearing's edge. The change had come over him quickly, as had his speed. He realized that he would need to slow down if he wasn't going to crash into his own defensive wall, feathered though he knew it to be. To slow down he drove his heels into the supple spongiform mushrooms and dug in hard. His body slowed at first, but it was not the body of a dancer, and he pitchforked face forward into the earth and the mushrooms piled high around him. He slowly lifted his head and his eyes saw what his screaming heart would not. These were not mushrooms, but a field of unploughed dead bats.

The dead bats' fur-grey mould was so close to his eyes that his field of vision was nothing but bursted blood bags of once tiny soaring beating hearts. Each one had been in a dying love compact with Sol. He lay still, and beyond the bats something moved towards him. Something and someone bent over and touched his head with two forefingers. His eyes moved beyond the closest bat and followed the fingers. Each was part of a pale ivory hand transcribed by fine lines of ridged silver red veins. And each vein oxbowed beyond the necklaced wrist and drew straight along alabaster arms. And as his eyes raised beyond they rested on green gold eyes each trained and unblinking on him. This was what he had been waiting for and planning and scheming for. This was the fruit of his labour. This was Sol. Two things had happened to him this day that had never happened before. He had laughed full of life, and he had feared full of death. He was no longer the Getto of yesterday. As he lay trembling on his bat bed, Sol touched him, then fixed him with a look of such radiance that all his lonely and inner cellar-stored evil evaporated in the love of her look.

In Polimnia Troia laid out a plan for housing and for defence, and for the storage of grain and wheat over the winter. The palisade had one main gate facing a clearing in front of the forest. Once inside this gate, which was defended at all hours by the best troops, you would immediately find yourself in gardens. This town was full of vegetables and fruit and flowers. The flowers were first, hanging over two broad benches either side of the gate. The first impression of this outpost was that inside the scent was of spring and renewal. Vegetables were arranged along deep stone counters sluiced with fresh running water. In every shadowed and cobbled lane of this warren of life, there was fresh fruit in market stalls on both sides of the road. Beyond this the town developed its beginnings of elegance and purpose. The buildings Troia commissioned were colonnaded and a simple but noble series of arched walkways provided relief and shade from the humid forest heat. At the very end of the town, and at the end of its straight avenue was Troia's town hall. Here he gathered all to think and discuss, to read and declaim, to act and dance.

Amongst his new friends was a four-limbed bearded and blind wordsmith. He was called Homer. And he spoke without cease. This was where in Polimnia Troia began to turn the forest into a place for a new race of noble beings, who would fight, yes, but who prized poetry and love and peace over the raw bite of the past.

Ordög had moved beyond the immediate confines of the mine as well. Though not too far. He liked the healing power of coal, and the balm and honey bee fertility of black. Black night, black dawn, black day, all enveloped by sweaty earth black stripes of banded black time: coal, coal, coal, and again coal. That's what everything was about. When he sat and thought of the things he thought about, he reduced all of the arguments into sets and subsets. All cubed into a hierarchical series of relationships between the motive force of one argument, and its loss of force and reason in the belly of another. Then one by one the arguments would give way, as the thought tree compressed to schools of thought, then branches of knowledge, then finally a single wind blown fallen leaf of an idea; the accumulated effect of all those causes: coal. So Ordög set up a camp near the mine.

One spider had escaped the treacle tart suicide in the attack on Troia's positions in the battle at the end of Ordög's world, and this was the great designer spider, onanist and hermaphrodite, Tamerlane. He would slowly grow in confidence, learning from his master, and help Ordög plan a counterattack, until he outdid him in bad, and even in the very little good that can be a fellow traveller of evil. This spider was truly the heir of the cleansing wind, the scourge of the steppes and the acid acme of the end of time. This was Tamerlane. And our story begins anew with him.

They talked and talked in those first weeks. Ordög orga-
nized everything, and at first just talked with Tamerlane
about why this, and why that. Soon though, he passed
along simple tasks, which Tamerlane scuttled off to do.
At the end of each day, as their camp grew, and as more
of the troops knew what to do with themselves, Ordög
would sit down with Tamerlane in the shade of a chip
black quarry of coal, and talk of their plans, and of
life, its challenges, satisfactions and failures. In one of
these conversations Tamerlane began to see the scope of
the possibilities in front of him, as well as the quality
of Ordög's mind. It was like drinking from a fire hose.
Late one night, very late, Tamerlane said to Ordög, 'But
why so much killing?' To which Ordög replied after long
thought, 'I guess it's the deaths that I like. Killing just
accelerates what happens in nature anyway.' He paused
again. 'But I need to know so much about death which is
unknown. And knowledge doesn't move in inspired leaps
of insight, it's a process of accumulation. It's like science
really. Think of a wave of pebbles inexorably crashing
on a beach of pebbles. Each pebble is a discreet idea and
experiment. But it only has force in the wave. It and its
millions of cohorts crash against other pebbles which had
been parts of earlier waves, and eventually the sheer mass

of moving mass tells. And then we know.' A longer pause followed, the shadows crept forward against the darkness. 'I need to harness all the power of coal. Coal is the answer to all questions when the questions finally get there, but coal is made up of millions of organic deaths, and I need to understand how to harness death to eventually mine coal faster.' Tamerlane understood and in those moments by the reflected darkness of a cold coal wall, he realized that to aim like Ordög for the greater good could transform a spider into a statesman.

Ordög continued the next night as an uncle might with his orphaned nephew. 'If I could be everywhere at once, Tamerlane, then I could be at every death at once. But I can't, so killing both brings the death to me, and does so in sufficient numbers to draw conclusions from.' But Tamerlane had watched him kill, and had seen a sort of pleasure which went beyond the spirit of enquiry, so he put that to him. 'I am an aesthete too', Ordög replied. 'I like things to look a certain way. I have always struggled with the aesthetics of the glory of man; I prefer the ideal of complimenting nature by copying its random disorder. So I like to praise the gods by killing fast, as nature does slowly.'

As Ordög fathered-forth Tamerlane in the broad church of creating a stifling polity based on coal, and filling needs and wants buckets, Troia was creating a society at Polimnia which was based on the communion of agricultural surpluses married to a noble mix of art and poetry and thought; a round table of wit and tolerance, a permissive city which would grow by not knowing what it was growing towards, a place of freedom. And Sol and her new redeemed partner Getto, and Papageno, were at the same time growing good, and growing love, growing happiness, and growing innocence, and peace and song, in the middle of the dark forest, where now plentiful light had opened its breach to the forest floor and humus fertilised the bloated bat bodies into ranks of luscious floral bulbs and buds, filling the world of fairies and birds and small miracles with the wild and crazed colour of hope.

Papageno had taken to the skies again like any windhover would if any windhover could. And Papageno could. Complete with his feathers he took to the air, and the air again took to him. But the days of his free falling flying were past. This was no longer another past in the Motherland. This was now, in the only place left. So he flew to look and see. The dark forest now had light and colour and song, all mixed with spring tubers and thorns crowned with red berries and black ones, blue berries and blood ones. Fruit hung heavy on bent boughs. And heavy hands picked it and ate its bubbled juice. The forest was reborn as rich thick topsoil sprung spring. But the forest still harboured its history. It had Getto in its creases and folds, and now it had Ordög and Tamerlane by its mine, and Troia by the edge of the sea. It was no longer all bad, but it was far from all good. So Papageno took to the sky and saw and looked. Every day he flew, looked, and flew back to the forest fortress. Here he would tell Sol what was happening and what he saw. So even here, in the cradle of innocence, where goodness couldn't brook bad, they saw and prepared for what they dreaded.

First he noticed all the activity at Polimnia. It was unmis-takable. A palisade was fast becoming a town rich in roofs, and towers. Streets paved with flat river stone began to splay outward from the main gate up the body of the town. Side streets acquired side paving, and awnings stretched shadow over the streets and market in the warm months. Day by day Papageno saw this change, and flew back to say what he saw. Closer to the mine he also saw work and activity built into the hills behind the seams of coal. Sol-diers hid when he was overhead, but he knew they were there. Sometimes he caught sight of the one they called Ordög. And recently he saw a large spider drilling cohorts through manoeuvres under the canopy. He saw all this, and flew back to say what he had seen. So Sol began to gather details of the growing planet, and she also began to grow herself from goddess to one who does, and one who can, and one who will. Every day she was less goddess and more woman. And this was just in time because Getto had fallen in love with her, and had thought he could see good in himself. Indeed he thought he was redeemed of all bad. But bad doesn't good itself easily. It goes down hard. And Getto felt more like Getto going down hard with it.

For once in his life Getto didn't slide along on base fear, nor impart fear to all comers. For days after, he lay in his lair in the heart of the transformed forest fortress and listened to Papageno fly in and out with words and tales of what was happening beyond them. Sol would note and move on to another bird, to be sure that here too feathers would be back and bright and beautiful. Where she walked, light would open a window, so as the days and then months passed the forest was no longer dark. New undergrowth sprouted and flowered where light had previously not fallen, and the forest floor became a carpet of colour and scent. In this new world humming birds and orioles joined the resident weavers and finches to create a chorus of nesting and breeding and coupling all around him. But in his bed Getto switched and swapped between wanting her love and wanting his old adamantine and hard travertine self.

On one morning of birdsong, Papageno came back from one of his encircling flights and told more to Sol and Getto of this spider he saw. This wasn't the first they had heard of the spider, and indeed a picture began to fill out of a confident martial and aggressive arachnid. Getto listened carefully to all the details. The spider was seen here, then there; with an impi of jack-boots, and without; side by side with Ordög, but mostly on his own. Each day the spider pushed his way further through trees and forest floor. Each day he was seen closer to Papageno's new home by Papageno above him. He was taking the measure of things, surveying the land, assaying the geology and geography of this world. And behind him, more slowly, his army too moved outward from its perch behind the mine. Ordög was always seen at the centre of the mine; never by the shore, occasionally in the trees, but mostly in its dark heart covered in coal dust and bathed in black light. But his world was rippling outwards from his stone stilled centre. At dawn Tamerlane marched and measured. And, from his perch above, Papageno watched and measured too, at sunset, the distance narrowing each day between a world of coal and one of light.

Getto had always been sly. He didn't always know what he wanted, but he always knew how to get to where what he wanted would be more than just one thing. And this time the two things that his sly shovel-full of brain wanted were opposites. One was good, and one not. Choosing bad would be the hoped-for long legacy of himself to posterity. The problem with good is that it never leaves the trace on life bad does. Bad always leaves a mark behind. And Getto was swooned by that. But he could wait to see which way to jump. Good too was possible for him. He had just felt love, and had recently hummed along to birdsong. He could discard a cardinal's red hat and opt easily for the Franciscan cowl. Getto was never a thinker, but a dreamer of deeds and greatness. If that came from sacrifice and a mendicant's life then let it, if from mendacity and the sacrifice of other's lives, then be. He could swim with fish or fly with birds.

But first he needed to know what bad was all about. He had always been bad's boon buddy. But his bad was local; domestic maybe. It was the sort of bad most of us will steer near before luck plucks us from its pull; bad with a white picket fence around it. Ordög's bad was regal and Olympian. And Tamerlane must have learned something of Ordög's plan. So having taken his own advice to be good for some little while now, Getto opted to find out whether bad might weigh more. Moral questions are fought out by weight, with a sabre thrust and cut. Only ethical questions are dull enough to require the light ballet of tip scoring foils. So off to the woods he went, sabre in hand, to find Tamerlane, meet Tamerlane, know Tamerlane, and find out what Tamerlane knew. In he went, at his ancient pace, no bloated bat bags to bubble him fast forward. Just his steady padded pace. He could meet Tamerlane where he liked; at his choosing. Nobody knew this ground like he did. So he carefully chose ground that suited him. Somewhere where he could surprise the spider enough to stand him still, but not enough to frighten him to flight or fight. And there he hunched and waited. And waited and waited. Until he heard the snap-crack of branch twig and leaf under the unbundling Prussian goose step of eight legs marching different ways in the same direction. And he suddenly felt more frightened than he ever intended Tamerlane to be.

Spiders don't stop on the spot, nor is their turning circle tight. Tamerlane came round a corner legs first and last. He saw what was ahead only once half of him was where ahead was. So he ran into Getto. Getto screamed under the jumble of bent black limbs. It was like being pinned down by several floors of collapsed scaffolding. He could breathe only when Tamerlane shifted his weight from one stuck leg stick to another. Slowly the spider unpicked each leg from its disjointed knot and raised himself above Getto. He knew who he was. Getto stammered his introduction and peace. So the spider stepped back, and Getto breathed. Then from his back foot Tamerlane, who had listened silently to Getto's overture, pivoted upwards and then downwards in one light footed lunge and sank his fangs deep into Getto's fat neck. Quickly Getto was immobilized by threads of hardening silk issued by wet glands. Then, when he was swaddled fast, Tamerlane said that he would continue his walk and be back for him later. 'Then I will listen. I don't have time now.' Just before leaving though, he nimbly lifted his vacuum packed prey and hung him swinging from a tree, only to head off and go where Getto had been. Strung up and tightly packed Getto watched him disappear from two tiny holes made in his silk mask.

As the breeze blew through the forest he swayed upside down from his branch like a ripening fat fruit. And the world too swayed as he looked out for help.

The day and next night clocked round and Getto swayed to and fro like a pendulum. And he thought and thought. Mostly about how to unravel his silky ribbon prison, but also about good and evil, and about Sol, and those beautiful birds with their palette of coloured feathers, and Papageno with his sung joy, and what about that sad tortoise he had trapped and abused, who had soared to the sky with Papageno, and more. He was feeling sorry for himself, and good rose like cream from his sour middle. So back and to, and forth and fro, he rocked and clocked and swung above. And thought and thought. And he thought about Ordög, his rival for evil, and Tamerlane, the apprentice. And he thought that only good would get him out of this pharaoh's swaddling. Bad would likely leave him stuck, and no longer keeping time with the rest of long life. So simply, he chose good again. It was out of necessity of course, but surely it should be. Good couldn't really claim to be there by rights because of any need for it before a need arose. So this simple fat slippery rubber glove of life chose good now, as he might choose bad later, and at sunset through the tiny breathing hole Tamerlane had left for him he prayed:

Take me Sunlight, for what I have given.
You make me nought Everlasting One.
Place me in the field, the garden, the flock of birds,
Or bid me not of Your things,
Forbidden Lip on Me.

And back and fro, and to and forth, he swung and swung,
and thought and thought.

Troia's Polimnia was King Arthur's Camelot, or Paris under the Abbé, or Rome under Augustus with Virgil standing scribe, or Florence while the Magnificent Lorenzo lived. It was all these: the confluence of time and a mind; of power built quickly, and spent slowly. In time wood turned to brick, and brick to stone. Troia too turned talk from words – then sums of words – to definitions, then sense; finally flight: poetry. But hold; not too quick. This is what happened; and in real time. Troia was a slow tortoise, not fast and loose, not a conqueror. Not Caesar, Julius, but Caesar, Augustus. He didn't happen to things, things happened to him. And Homer, his friend, sang of these things. And they happened because he sang of them. Soon trees lined the streets and Polimnia was bathed in grid beams of sunlit city space. Pine trees began to draw the town out to the country; and pine needles pointed paths from one pine to another, then to all pines and to all points of Polimnia's growing country compass.

Troia had been hard at work making half-men from the bestial soup of cartilage, blubber and bone at his side. This wasn't easy. For a tortoise it was a supreme effort, and the only thing he did which is with us today. That's not entirely true, Polimnia is still with us, but spread wide under shopping centres and warehouse corrugation. Pine trees have been incorporated into public parks and some marble facades still dress the streets. But the making of man and the making of a mind for man which could reach beyond bloodlust and hoarding was this tortoise's legacy. He made them every day. They were unformed first, then formed anew. They were godfathered by Homer's song and poetry at the dinner table, and mothered by battle and war in the field and the forest. They evolved. Troia didn't. Troia stayed forever and ever a tortoise whilst this plastic change happened, and what was half once was whole now. Together he and his new men thought and fought. But Troia's great friend in life-making was Homer. Homer drank with him, built with him, stood by him in his final illness, and then when he was no more, told his tale. And of the making of us.

So sing muse, of Earth and its making. Let the Earth too sing its sunken song of waking. And Homer sang of Troia and the first men of Polimnia. He sang of this early tribe in the lee of the woodland, and of the sea which pressed upon them. And he sang of their deeds with stone, and of their bronze weapons. He also brought forth the tale of Ordög and his warehouse world, and of Sol and the Motherland. And he sang too of Papageno as Papageno would soon sing of him. Homer's singing wasn't for posterity, wasn't for us in the future to hear and follow with a knowing nod and a metered tap the past deeds of heroes. He sang for them then, of their hearts and swords, that very morning of the waking world. He sang to put mettle in them if they flagged, and courage when it failed. He sang side by side with them as they fought and died. He cheered them with a huzzah as they charged a redoubt, and they turned and cheered him too for cheering them. This was the world, and these were the men Troia built in those early days on earth. But I am going ahead of myself and have left behind the story of the first battle amongst the pines, and of what it foretold of the fates of all of our friends, and the destiny of those whose names still stalk our fear today.

It was more a first contact, a skirmish, and it happened at Ordög's bridge. The bridge had been built by Ordög's engineers but wasn't near his mine. Nor was it close to Polimnia. It was in-between, and spanned a chasm which, though not formally marking a boundary, marked the change in landscape and geology which defined the different peoples. Homer and Tamerlane for different reasons and in different ways made their way to opposite ends of the span on the same day. One was all legs, and one all tales. Initially courtesy prevailed; even interest. Homer – warm at first, and to the last – liked this gangly and ungainly spider. Tamerlane never liked anyone, but liked the universal deception of like. So he entertained this bearded tale teller, and told his own tale. And there they stood, in the middle of the narrow breadth of the long span of the ribbon bridge, over the deepest gorge. And they talked. Homer talked of Troia and Polimnia, and he spoke for hours.

As the sun rose to the middle above them he talked and talked. Whilst talking he smiled, gesticulated, and stroked his great black beard as if pulling more tales out from within it. And Tamerlane listened all buttoned up and cautious, as if he was waiting for the other penny to drop. Nothing dropped, but eventually Homer stopped. Tamer-lane now briefly told of Ordög, and the coal. He smiled when talking; a neat smile, contained at its corners. Just as Homer spoke of Troia like the best of all knights, so too did Tamerlane when talking of Ordög. And this was no carnival of appearance. He really did love and idolize his father figure and thoughtful killer, Ordög.

But eventually the tales moved apart and could not be bridges between the two types of opposite ends of kind. One story was about power exercised with a million razor blades, to cut out what couldn't lead to coal and more power, and the other was about power lightly shod, and reluctant of use. And this was a young Homer, before his understanding of kin and kind. This was before Agamemnon, before the rage of Achilles and the strength of Ajax, before Hector and the stubborn walls of Troy. This was a green Homer, and Tamerlane knew it. So, in the mid-sentence of another of Homer's mid-sentences, Tamerlane looped under the bridge, and then over it, wrapping a silken thread fully round Homer's ankles as a vaquero might bring down a steer in the Pampas. Homer fell and then slid over the bridge's narrow ledge to hang upside down over the gorge, with only one foot caught between the bridge planks holding him above a fall below to death.

The men on his side of the bridge saw and closed fast to the middle. Faster than the troops on the other side. Tamerlane had to hurry, and so he began to cut cord in a wild whirr. Even with eight legs he was no match for an armed platoon of well trained men, particularly as he had to cut, and defend himself as well as hold on to the super-structure of the swaying bridge. As the last ropes frayed apart he scuttled back fast leaving Homer and Troia's troops flailing in mid-air. The soldier closest to Homer cut away at the silk thread holding Homer to the bridge. And in hacking at this he inadvertently axed at the last strands of rope holding the bridge together.

The sound of the unravelling hemp was like that of an onrushing train, and the bridge was no longer suspended, but fell from space like a broken clapboard house in the eye of a hurricane. Everything went this way and that. Men rained down the gorge, hitting the ground where its slope was still steep, thus leaving broad stripes of blood and bone in abstract daubs at pretty angles to the blue and white cataract of river racing by. Those unlucky enough to have lost balance first fell furthest, and didn't leave behind a splayed paint tube of body bag on the landscape, but jack-knifed like kingfishers into the rapids, surfacing only further down as opened sacks of gutted life. The man who had rushed to Homer's side fared no better. His momentary saviour and clumsy comrade flew backwards through the too little time before death in a gorgeous slow studied reverse rotation, with his bronze axe leading his body's martial muscle in a last lament to brawn and beauty. He hit the ground where it was flat, at terminal velocity.

The sound was like thunder, and still reverberates through space today, still wakes children under their eaves and covers and starts them into fear. These are sounds heard but hard to write of. If you can't hear it, see it. It was like the ploughing open of a whale's belly as it is winched aboard a whaling ship; it was like that deep layer of black cloud on the horizon which sailors know will orphan their children; it was an ancient stand of trees felled, a proud bull elephant brought to its knees by the report of a heavy gun; it was the bell tolling for us; the deep double bass of the world's end. That's what it sounded like.

But Homer hung on; and lived. Enough of Tamerlane's sticky silk stuck to him to keep him from following his friends down south. The section of the bridge he held on to struck the cliff, and snapped the sky, like a lion tamer's whip. He shot this way and that; and was lucky. Very lucky. Others died on that bridge, pancaked below. But Homer lived, and with Troia fought to settle good and right, beauty and song, in sad black sick broken ur-acres of heedless space. He hung on that day, and for many thousands of days after, to create with Troia a reason why, and the first tale and fable that made the blood worth running, for all the laughter and love that could run with it.

Troia called his worthy men to his side when Homer's dispatch was sounded of the dead at Ordög's bridge. Troia was always primed for peace, but life had taught him that war would wait for nobody, nor would it want a cause, or booty, or even a pragmatic living space. War wanted war, and if it took its neighbour's peace in the reckoning, then peace be damned.

So war began here too, as it had ended in Ordög's land. Tamerlane was an orthodox strategist, and built his line of battle around numbers and blind obedience and discipline. Ordög for now let his pupil bring the fight to Troia. He watched his inky step-spider with pride, and shed tears thinking of what his first faltering kill would mean to him. This helped him hope for the future. As Tamerlane left their war council, Ordög clutched him by a leg and said, 'death is vainglorious. Let her preen by you.' The supply lines were short, the internal lines of communication taut. The marching clipped, over flint, dirt, and cobble, but there was little verve and initiative in these marching clones. They moved forward because Tamerlane willed it, and because physics slipped the earth equally and oppositely under their boots. One day, perhaps, you might read and learn what the limits of tyranny are. But here and now, and then, all you had to do was march to your death in Tamerlane's army.

Troia called his knights to his side and they too counselled of war. Some for, some not. But after all the arguments were spent, what was left was Polimnia, and their families, and fear. Troia asked his best knights to organize a classic defence, and to stockpile food and water. The forward lines would be under the billowing umbrella pines on the plain between the outer walls and the forest. Everyone else would be within. Everyone except for Homer, and this sly tortoise.

First they had to organize their disguises, in case they were stopped by Tamerlane's pickets. Homer looked too much like a big bearded bard to blink past a glance. Troia, however, was the real problem. Everyone knew that a tortoise was standing toe to toe against Ordög. Of course it helped that Troia no longer had a hard shell to be spotted by. All the same, his appearance outside a hard shell was so unique that stopping him for questioning, went without question. Troia wasn't a master of disguise like the Scarlet Pimpernel. He wasn't even particularly self-conscious. He had unerring judgement, an ear for verse and song, an eye for a battlefield, and speech that could raise the dead. But he looked like a balloon as the air fizzes out. So this odd couple tried masks, wigs, colours and creams, to look less odd. Nothing worked. Eventually they hit on a deception which would hide them both completely. A horse hide in sections was stitched together, and housed Homer in front and Troia behind. Scrummed front to back, they were tethered to a carriage behind them, and bound axle and brace to a real horse. Thus these two clod-hopped clumsily towards the front lines, and beyond.

Not far into clod-hopping on fast forward, Troia, who had to keep time with the real horse, weakened in the dark stench of the faux horse. He popped his head out at the centre stitch, roughly where pregnancy would billow. As he did this their carriage passed the first of Ordög's pickets and the first inquirer queried. Surprisingly two heads answered the dumb question; one a horse's, and one a tortoise's head from the equine's belly. Things would have worked if the two species had agreed their answers. But these comrades in capers hadn't. One, the poet, said 'horse', and one, the tortoise, said 'horse too'. Now, pregnancy can produce much of this and that, even little, like immaculate little. But one horse answering twice 'horse', to an 'are you a horse' question, must be a horse's ass. And to this simple sentry this horse's ass seemed like two horses' asses. Troia suddenly realized that his head was in the way of his brain, and withdrew it. Back inside his curiosity got the better of him, and he looked back with one eye through the horse's ass. As he did this the sentry was rounding the very back of this odd quadruped. Here he peered lasciviously at the horse's backside. And the backside peered back.

Instinct thought quicker than thinking, and Troia thrust his stumpy arm out of the horse's ass, grabbed the stunned sentry by the neck, and pulled him into the same inside of the horse he and Homer were sharing. The space inside a horse – even an empty one – is less than a look from the outside would suggest. Homer was almost immediately pushed far forward into the neck and head of this nag. To steady himself, and keep the head off the ground he thrust his arms through the nag's nostrils, and perambulated forward. Troia instead hung like a foal ready to drop in the mare's belly. And the sentry, who was inside but wanted to be outside, thrust his arms out through the much abused horse's posterior, and pushed and pulled in the opposite direction to Homer at the front. The real horse of course moved ahead, whilst this fabric roan moved everywhere at once. In this fashion they appeared and passed the second and last sentry, who was too frightened to stop their weird progress. When they eventually crested the ridge on the far side of the plain, they stopped, and flopped out of their Trojan bean bag. The sentry was tied up with what was left of the horse's tail, and a bemused, and slightly ashamed pair of heroes, silently moved on, into the dark forest. Just so, Achilles.

Inside the forest our two recent thespians judged their march by skill and bravado. But this forest had buried many such ill-equipped explorers. And soon, like many of them, they were hopelessly lost. At first this was exciting. Homer boasted, as only a poet might, that being lost was timeless, liberating, and the very start of the human condition. He then went on to praise being found also as timeless, liberating, and the beginning of the human condition. All of this as they tramped fruitlessly on the forest floor. Troia said less, but kept his ears trained on the rich canvas of woodland sounds around them. On they tramped, tripped and stumbled, on branch, root, twig and stump. Deeper and further they sallied and sailed through strong currents of moving matter and heaving forest floor, and a humid noxious torrent of weaving teeming insect gore. Their painted faces and daubs of cream were soon replaced by bites and sores, by cuts and scrapes, much blood, and more. They tacked, this way now, and stayed the course. Then that way, and stayed that course too. Then, this again. Then, that. Above them, beside them, and beneath them, the forest raged, and in its deep, rich, hot, and wet green grip, Homer and Troia were tossed and turned, then finally sunk, upturned, and lost.

Water wasn't the problem, nor was food. The forest provided both. For anyone lost, madness is what waits upon you. Everything on life's tally stick of events makes sense, however bad. But not being lost. Being lost is dizzying first, desperate second, and mad, mad, mad, after and forever. Troia and Homer were in the first dizzying phase. They circled the same paths, circled trees they had circled before, and now circled each other. They spoke to each other, and early on even listened to each other. Now they listened no more, and whispered to themselves. They prayed. Then they waited, shouted, stopped, listened. Nothing. Just the forward creep and volume of breathful forest life. They prayed loudly; shouted to the gods. And listened back. Nothing. Then they forsook the gods, and all the wonder of the stitching together of light and dark, and the deep plaintive singing in the warm sleeved folds of the unfolding universe. They named all the good things in plenty's cornucopia, and then they forsook these too, each by each. When they had finished, there was nothing left, so they damned the gods. And now they entered the second phase: desperation. The first night fell.

Huddled together and bound now to a night on the forest floor they tried to close their eyes and sleep. Perhaps they did briefly. But the clammy cold pushed through on to their bones and kept shaking them awake. Homer's teeth clattered and ground like an involuntary mortar and pestle. Troia's eyes froze open looking out and up through a clearing in the canopy. Space is cold, and for all its hot stars seemed then to be no more than a spring sown field deadened by a late frost. Troia stared down at the stars, only held from falling ever downwards to an icy death by gravity's pin. This night seemed full of endings. The end of day, the end of hope, the end of the two of them, the end of Polimnia. Troia lay thinking and watching the dark maw of the universe swallow all of his hopes of beginnings. Next to him Homer mumbled fragments of language. One eyed giants contended the future of every-thing with unmatched men. Rivers burned, and civiliza-tions died of love. Boats left nowhere, and were wrecked on nowhere's rocks. They were both delirious.

As the black blackened, Troia blacked out. Homer too was quiet. Maybe the quiet of ever took him. Or not. Troia couldn't know now. The night that is always ever was more than ever now. Shallow ink lapped the light edge of evening, where evening still stalled, and then rippled waves of inkfall fell over the last light. Troia's eyes were still frozen open. Blind and black too. His mind had long gone, and no longer held his lucky trove of treasure near. Like space itself he was just another fast moving but stock-still bundle of cooling heat; a transfer of energy from something we know but muse about, to something we can muse on but will never know. And then, as the black turned to grey, and then to yellow, and orange after, he saw something. It seemed like no more than movement above. Maybe something alive again in him. But as he strained to see, he saw more. Things circled the heavens above; objects. They weren't space things, like meteorites, or comets. They were things that were of us, and if they weren't of us now, they would be. One of them was like a stele, but he saw it as an obelisk. Another was not one thing but two, strong tall bronze warriors. As light returned and day swapped night's disfavour he saw images too: a nude woman of warm skin tones, all human, all a picture of how things are when they are as they are, against the abstract grey stone background of a palace; the world as it isn't, wedded to the world as it is. Heart and curve and blood and body, lying down with mind and line and reason. He woke finally. His body warmer. He woke Homer too. And as the last day-lit painting flew by they followed its sky-trail to safety.

Homer was the first to spot it. They were in a clearing. And just off-centre in this clearing was a tree. Hanging from a branch was a sizeable silken pod. Two eyes stared out from inside the pod, and a voice from inside was whispering, 'forgiven with dreaming, the stamen, the fool'. It took a while to cut Getto out, but they did, and he belly flopped to the ground. He was given water and berries. They sat him up and listened to his story. As he told it he realized that it was without embellishment. He hadn't added heroism, or moral choice against long odds. He was telling the truth about his abandonment of Sol and Papageno, and the truth about his search for Tamerlane. He told the truth about his weakness for wrong, and the boredom he found in right. And in telling the truth, he found that there was something about it that freed him from the linked chain of lies he had always relied on. Troia and Homer listened to him, but didn't understand what just telling this story was doing to Getto. They were of those beings to whom the truth was not a choice, and didn't understand what a healing balm the truth can be to a jaundiced life liar. Again, Getto felt new and free, just as he had when Sol touched him on his spongy bed of bats all those mornings ago.

Homer helped Getto to his feet, and as the day began to lose its hard edge and the soft light dappled down through the trees, they walked to what was once Getto's forest fortress. Above the trees, birds filled the evening sky with song. Wind currents swayed the tree tops. Leaves, petals, and feathers drifted here and there. As they reached the outer walls of the forest fortress, the day's light ran ahead of them, and ran ahead of dusk falling in behind their little marching column, and ran up the mottled bark of a thousand swaying tree trunks, as it had run down them that dawn. The last light lit the tallest trees, and their top-gallants reflected it back like a semaphore to a star, before it sank beneath the horizon. Homer and Getto opened the gate and made their way inside to be welcomed first by Papageno, then Sol.

Sol felt something different about Getto right away. She sensed that he may have finally won his see-saw battle with himself. Before she greeted the others she embraced him, and as dusk turned to dark and the forest turned quiet Getto quietly cried in her arms. They all then made their way to Sol's tree house. Here they ate and drank. And here they talked and planned the coming battle. Troia had come thinking he would struggle to steel Sol and Papageno to a fight, but there was no struggle. They too knew that peace couldn't fight for them; only war could help them now, and only if they fought together could they win the long peace they prayed for. Troia also had counted on having Getto for a rival, but now he was at their side, and of them. They knew they may all die on the morrow, they knew what was at stake for history and for us, but that night, high up in Sol's tree house, they were a happy crew.

When the food was gone, and only the wine left, they let matters of battle and the tactics of the field fade. In its dread stead they drained the drink, and sang the songs they knew, which Sol led. Her voice was new here; unheard by earth, and by its birds. Unheard too by Troia and Homer, who each judged song as life alone without body. They sang themselves, and kept a tune from gracelessness, but when, that late warm dark night, Sol let her first breath lip her first sung earth note, they sat still, every one of them moved but unmoving, each now an inside poem of the life-giving earth. Each was tuned to her high range, and each in turn could add their bass to bring the gods down from up, to have them tread their feet here just now, at least in song, if not in deed. And as they sang the sleeping birds awakened, and though they didn't sing with Sol's song, but sang this bird to that, and that to another, each a birdsong of its own, the whole was now more than a way for gods to walk with us, it was life beyond even them, the answer that morning, as the forest floor was lit by dawn.

Without sleep they gathered thick in the central square. More birds lined the town walls, and thronged the trees along the main thoroughfare. Troia then spoke.

'Nothing is more troubling than the end. Look at it; death, the end of days, and the end of love. We know today that all of that is as might be, that all we love may not outlive this day. We know there is no mass that we can exchange for security, no gold or silver that can buy our peace and hold it. And we know that tonight we may not see dusk, and that from tomorrow's dawn our homes may never again house us. But now, right now, we are here in this world of trees, and sun, and wind, and rivers that run to seas, and seas that rise and fall like a beating heart. We have goblins, hobgoblins, monsters and satyrs, we have good and bad and great and small; we have me for now, we have you, forever, I pray. But above all, we have hope. Tomorrow can wait.'

Then it was Sol's turn: 'From today this city will for-ever be known as Urbania, for we are the light of reason. I cannot fight for you, for I cannot fight. But I can invest you with enough of me to help you as you fight for all of us. So today I need you to be you a little bit longer, then, should you live or die, you can be me.' And as one the birds lifted to the sky beyond.

Tamerlane hadn't been idle in the days leading to the battle. With Ordög he had arranged their forces and looked for the ground to give them advantage where it could. Ordög now doted on him, but his love was never divorced from his interest. There was a reason he had pocketed one spider to make the long voyage here while all the others ended up as goo and shoe polish. Tamerlane could procreate on his own. More than anything this was what was needed of him now. So he begat fast, and his eggs begat past him, then theirs past them. Soon the coal black hillsides, roads, quarries and collieries of their industrial estate were carpet covered in the silken white gauze of millions of pulsating spider eggs. And as each spat out its hairy black ejaculate, the hillsides and roads merged black again; then again sex and egg; then egg white whisked landscape, and the spill of a million soft shells at once, before black again swarmed over white.

Unlike men spiders didn't need training to be effective. It helped, of course, but what really mattered was sheer mass. It was like a plague of locusts. Nothing could stand in their way. And in their wake, nothing could stand at all. Fire was the only force that could channel them. But with these numbers it couldn't be the charnel house it was before.

Ordög had coal ferried in strips leading from him to his bridge. These strips were on either side of the road. The bridge over the gorge was gone. But this no longer mattered. Men didn't need to cross; spiders did. Early on the morning of battle, as Sol still sang, Ordög lit his fuses. The roadsides lit up into a gauntlet of fire, and at their head Tamerlane opened the spigot of spiders. As a river they heaved and crashed and shouldered over rises, and gathered momentum downhill. Then, as they came to a corner, or needed to breast a hill, they gathered together again, a roiling river of black legs. At the gorge, where the remains of the bridge work lay, they didn't pause. Over the sides of the sheer wall they poured. The sentries posted at the other side were too far to distinguish what it was that poured over the opposite cliff face. It seemed like a pure stream of unfaceted black; oil maybe. They watched the headwaters hit the gorge floor, and felt real fear when they saw that the liquid didn't follow the gorge down, but crossed without a crease in its order and line, and now the river reached their cliff face, and up it flowed. The first sentries of Troia's army stayed to stem this teeming upriver jet black spider split-end from cresting onto the plains. They quickly improvised. From well above they dropped burning balls of pitch and tar over the side, and onto leaping headwaters. These punched craters of fire into the spider mass, like sun spots against the dark universe. One after another of these balls was lit and lifted over the edge, and for a time they slowed the spiders' march. This gave the forces along the edge of the gorge time to retreat to the second line of defence, much closer to Polimnia. It also allowed them to set light to the country behind them. The heather and dry summer grasses burnt quickly. The pine trees took more time to join the fray, but once flames reached their resinous sap they burst like grenades across the toasted earth. Pine after pine smoked and then exploded in a fireball of flying syrup. At this point the first spiders seeped onto the plain. And at the same moment Troia, Sol, Getto, Papageno and Homer hurried in through Polimnia's gate.

From the turrets Troia and Papageno spied the distant black line through smoke and fire. It began as a ribbon of crepe on the horizon, like a border lining a printed death notice. Then it heaved to thicker, then fat black. Red eyes could now be seen by them as well, but only on the spiders riding above their burnt and boiled brethren. Explosions littered the field, blowing spiders in parts hither and thither. Troia asked Papageno to fly over the advancing front line and look for Tamerlane. He also reminded him to hold the birds back until he gave him the command. Tamerlane too pulled up his forces and clambered up a tower of spiders – most dead, some alive – to spy Polimnia in the distance. A relay of runners messaged between him and Ordög. Back in the safety of his quarry Ordög revelled in the news of the burning plain, and the crackling pines. He revelled too in the aesthetics of the road of dead spiders. He sent a message back to his step-spider asking him to hold the line long enough for him to get there and survey the scene. Tamerlane held the line and waited. Above him Papageno saw what was happening. Saw Tamerlane pull up. Saw Ordög being carried on an anthracite litter towards the gorge. He saw Ordög stop shy of the cliff edge and look down at the black stalagmite of death. He saw Ordög call for brush and paper, and essay some thinly applied colour.

And then he watched him lowered over the edge in a basket, all the time quick and light with his brush and his mood and his manner. Across the gorge floor he skipped over the cooling tar, stopping here and there to add details at a stroke. At the facing wall on the gorge's other side he stopped in wonderment and stared for some time at the deep channels created in the spider gore by the burning balls of pitch thrown from above. It looked like a biological cutting, a freeze frame of life interrupted. Here an eye, there one looking back, legs once in motion now fossils on his causeway. He loved what he saw. Papageno saw what Ordög loved, and flew back over Tamerlane to Polimnia.

Papageno relayed his story and Troia called for the birds. He wouldn't normally play his only card so early in the set, but his horror of Ordög unbalanced him. And of a sudden a million birds flew over Tamerlane. Ordög looked up at the same time and saw them coming. He sat; looked over the gorge, marked his canvas again, once. Then he looked up again at all the feathered colour of blooming life alive, and cut his wrists open. He had reached his beauty. Tamerlane watched this unfold, and spoke swiftly to his progeny. As one they fell on Ordög and devoured him as he bled. Soon he was just them, a silhouette of spiders shaped like him. Then he was gone. His last words, which Tamerlane heard him whisper, were:

I brought you fuel,
I brought you black.
I am Ordög of steel, Ordög of coal, Ordög of the night.
I am Ordög, always, and I will be back.

With Ordög dead, Tamerlane had to decide whether to press on in his stead, or bide his time. It was a difficult decision as his blood was up, but Tamerlane knew that he bided time well. Why kill half the world, and risk being in that number, if he could just quietly befriend Troia, kill him, and have half the world without the gamble? He would do this. But he would not lay his arms down, or retreat without a show of strength. With his millions of spiders lining the horizon and each stamping each foot, a cloud of dust raised above the spiders, above the plain, and then above the sun which darkened this corner of the planet. On the far side of the plain Troia, Homer, Sol, Getto and Papageno, shivered as the sunlight died and a wind came towards them, and towards Polimnia. Soon all they could see was a beating breathing dust cloud, which sat at the gates of the city, stretched across the land, and pressed down on them from above. All the time the millions of legs beat out their drummer boy march. The whole world was now just a postage stamp of shrinking space under a cloud of noise and dust. All of a sudden the drumming ceased. All the noise and all the sound of all the world stopped, and was silent. A minute passed. Two. Three. Life held its last breath. And then out of the cloud curtain and in front of the gate stepped Tamerlane.

Black against brown. A silhouette of bad against the velvet of endless dust. Black in sharp relief. Eight black shafts, metallic, not matt, shifted out. All was quiet. All still. Tamerlane waited. The others too. Slowly the dust settled. Mote by mote the curtain rose downwards, from high above to low below. Still pulsing, but shrinking, the dust cloud settled on itself. The sun appeared again, though now in a far corner of the day sky. The world was back from brown now. Shards of blood red evening sky shot across Polimnia's bows, and, in front of her proud prow on the black earth, black spiders and a jet black Tamerlane began to hum as one. At first it was as quiet as the silence that preceded it, then by degree it wasn't. Ultrasonic turned sonic, then sound; then a shiver of all the air. Finally a deep vibration built from inside out, from bass to tender tenor. The red sky darkened as the last of daylight slipped over the horizon. And now, in the cold crisp starlight, a million spiders together hummed one long final note that brought the vibration of everything outside to everyone inside, and left it there long after they stopped. Tamerlane bowed to the five figures on the ramparts above him, and said, 'all this is yours: Earth, song, and spiders'.

Now Sol descended from the ramparts, the gate was opened, and she went alone to greet Tamerlane. She said,

We fly on sound
As cups are stringed with words.
Most of music squares our balance
In nature thus.
Even runs,
Angle stops, and
Round slips on
Alabaster.
There the periwinkled
Middle-ear catches
All, whispering God
Unto its master.

Then she sang, and with her a million birds sang too. Though dark now, the birds flew high enough to catch one last ray of sunlight, and the dark canvas of all our ancient night fears burst into a thousand coupling colours. Papageno flew highest and flew best. His fast flight took him past the dark earth, past the first gloom, past the lightening sky, past the carnival march of colour, past the ether, and pierced the little envelope we prosper in. He pierced it once on the way out to let Sol's voice reach the gods beyond us, and pierced it a second time coming back to equalize the pressure so that we could never follow her voice to the gods.

Thus man and woman settled here. On Earth, as above. With the gods gifts circling us, but within reach, for us to harvest. And our gift – our song – for the gods.

So now, when you look up at birds, or down at spiders, know that you are looking at yourself. For they fought and died for us and Earth. Today they fly and crawl for them-selves, as we build and blather for ourselves. But never for-get, when you lie down in darkness and close your eyes for sleep, that in each of us is a bird, and a spider too. And as sleep begins to best you, whisper the names of those who then willed us forward, 'Papageno, Troia, Sol, Homer, Getto and Tamerlane'. Don't whisper Ordög's name, and never ever speak it. Just those five names, Papageno, Troia, Sol, Homer, Getto and Tamerlane. Then dream.

AFTERWORD

I know this book is unusual. It would be convenient to be able to say it is a book that fits a ready-made genre well. Is it a book for children or young adults? Is it a fantasy for adults? Perhaps it's a sort of morality play, or a carnival of animals dressed up in a prose poem. Whatever it is, it is not obvious to me.

Generally when somebody writes a book they are not asked why they wrote it, and if they are, it's not always a good sign. Many of the few people who have read this book have asked me just that. I have assumed they meant 'why' in the sense of 'what made you', not 'how could you'.

Part of an answer is straightforward, I had no plan for the book, indeed I didn't know I was writing one. One day I wrote the first paragraph, and it was enough to make me want to write another one the next day. Soon the characters began to have a hold on me and I couldn't wait to find out what happened next. That's straightforward.

Another answer is less obvious, but that doesn't mean there is less truth to it, in fact there may be more.

The line that separates good from evil has always interested me. Is it a fixed bright line which separates moral absolutes, or is it a path between cultural artefacts that changes as you negotiate it? I remember many years ago reading Alan Bullock's great book on Hitler and Stalin. What made them history's twin tyrants? Why them? Why even write about them together? Is the psychology of a tyrant always the same, and does it always manifest itself in the same need to control all possible outcomes, the easiest route to which is death? And most importantly what makes Hitler nice to his dog? What makes Stalin such good company? My book is far from a book of answers to these questions, but I felt whilst it began to take shape, that today, when the lessons of the last world war are remembered less and less, and a fierce keening for a strong man grows everywhere, that I wanted fiction to help me get closer to what I was afraid of.